Little Red Riding Hood

Retold by Rob Lloyd Jones
Illustrated by Lorena Alvarez

Once upon a time there was a little girl called Little Red Riding Hood.

She loved how her ruby red cloak swished and swayed as she skipped around her bedroom.

Little Red Riding Hood lived by a creaky old forest, where her mother kept bees...

...and her father chopped down trees.

One day, Little Red Riding Hood's mother gave her a pot of honey.

"Will you take this to Grandma?"

Birds swooped
and chirped as
Little Red Riding Hood
skipped happily
through the trees.

"Hello, Little Red Riding
Hood," called her father.
But someone else was
watching her too...

A WOLF!

The wolf licked his lips and wagged his tail as he thought about eating Little Red Riding Hood for lunch.

He could have followed her and gobbled her up, but this was a cunning and crafty wolf, who loved to sneak around and set clever traps.

Snickering and snarling,
the wolf laid a large net
on the path between
the trees.

His tail twitched as
Little Red Riding Hood
skipped closer and closer...

...and skipped
right over the net.

Mumbling and muttering,
the wolf dug a deep hole,
and covered it with sticks
and leaves.

His eyes bulged, as
Little Red Riding Hood
skipped closer and closer...

...and skipped
right over the hole.

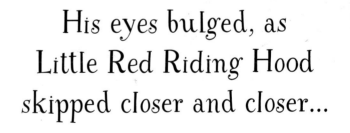

The wolf had one last plan. Grinning and
giggling, he crept to Grandma's cottage,
and knocked on the door.

He waited...

and waited...

...and then gobbled Grandma up in one hungry gulp. "Deeeelicious!" the wolf chortled. "Now for the main course."

The wolf's grin grew wider as he pulled on Grandma's clothes and leaped into her bed. "I'm so crafty!" he chuckled. "I'm the cleverest creature in the forest."

He waited... and waited...
until Little Red Riding Hood skipped into the cottage.

"Hello Grandma," said Little Red Riding Hood.
"I've brought you some honey."

Little Red Riding Hood came closer.

"Oh Grandma, what **big** ears you have."

"All the better to **hear you** with, my dear," said the wolf.

"Oh Grandma, what **big** eyes you have."

"All the better to **see you** with, my dear."

"Oh Grandma, what **big** hairy hands you have."

"All the better to **hug you** with, my dear."

Little Red Riding Hood stepped back.
"Um... Grandma, what **big** teeth you have."

"All the better to **eat you** with!" snarled the wolf.

Hooting and howling, the greedy wolf burst from the bed and swallowed Little Red Riding Hood in one enormous gulp.

With a full tummy and
a happy smile, the wolf fell
into a deep and dreamy sleep.

He didn't see
Little Red Riding Hood's
father at the window.

With a mighty roar,
Little Red Riding Hood's
father stormed into
the cottage.

He chopped open the wolf's
tummy, and Little Red
Riding Hood and Grandma
came tumbling out.

Now, Grandma had a cunning and crafty plan too...

Little Red Riding Hood gathered stones from outside,
and dropped some into the wolf's tummy.

Then Grandma
stitched his
tummy up.

When the wolf woke,
he howled and howled and
howled again. Each time
he moved, the stones
rattled inside him.

"I'll never be able
to sneak around and set
cunning traps," he moaned,
as he fled back to the forest.

Now all the wolf could eat were worms and beetles and slow little bugs.

He was never cunning or crafty again.

Gotcha!

And Little Red Riding Hood skipped
all the way home.

About the story

Little Red Riding Hood was first written down around 200 years ago, by brothers Jacob and Wilhelm Grimm, who lived in Germany. They collected lots of other well-known tales, including *Sleeping Beauty* and *Snow White*.

Edited by Lesley Sims
Designed by Laura Nelson

First published in 2016 by Usborne Publishing Ltd., Usborne House, 83-85 Saffron Hill,
London EC1N 8RT, England. www.usborne.com Copyright © 2016 Usborne Publishing Ltd.

This book belongs to:

_____

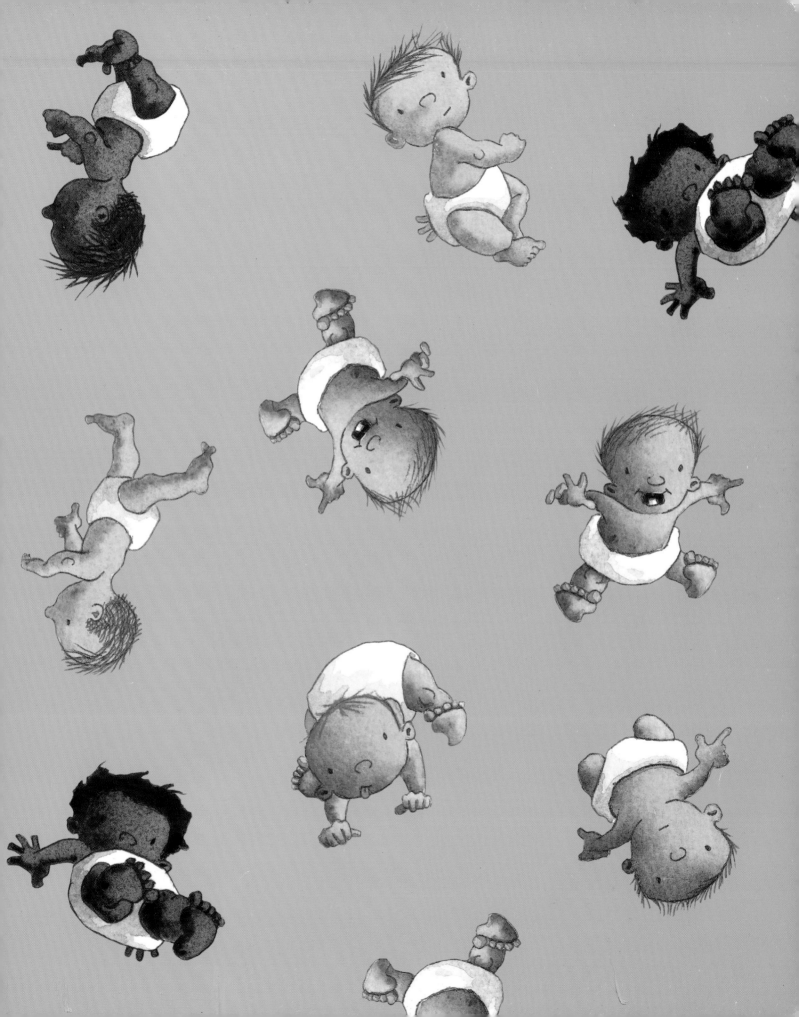

For Tilly — J.W.

For Amelie, Arlo, Magali, Phoebe, Sam and Tom — A.R.

This paperback first published in 2014 by Andersen Press Ltd.
First published in Great Britain in 2013 by Andersen Press Ltd.,
20 Vauxhall Bridge Road, London SW1V 2SA.
Published in Australia by Random House Australia Pty.,
Level 3, 100 Pacific Highway, North Sydney, NSW 2060.
Text copyright © Jeanne Willis, 2013.
Illustration copyright © Adrian Reynolds, 2013.
The rights of Jeanne Willis and Adrian Reynolds to be identified as
the author and illustrator of this work have been asserted by them in
accordance with the Copyright, Designs and Patents Act, 1988.
All rights reserved.
Colour separated in Switzerland by Photolitho AG, Zürich.
Printed and bound in Malaysia by Tien Wah Press.

10   9   8   7   6   5   4   3   2   1

British Library Cataloguing in Publication Data available.
ISBN 978 1 78344 103 7

UPSIDE DOWN BABIES

JEANNE WILLIS
ADRIAN REYNOLDS

ANDERSEN PRESS

Once when the world tipped upside down.

The earth went blue and the sky went brown.

All the baby animals tumbled out of bed

And ended up
with very funny mums instead.

Piglet went **ker-plonk** in a parrot's nest.

Porky and pink with no feathers on his chest.

"What a funny baby, no matter how I try,"
Mummy Parrot said, "this chick won't fly!"

Tortoise made a **splash!** in a big blue lake,

Shelly and scaly and bald as a snake.

"Whatever shall I do with a kid like him?"
Mummy Otter said. "This pup won't swim!"

Lion Cub fell in a field on his head,
"Eat up your grass, dear," Mummy Cow said.

The cub got cross and stamped his feet,
"I'm a carnivore!" he roared.

Baby Bunny
bounced
into Squirrel's drey,
He clung
to a branch
with his claws
all day.

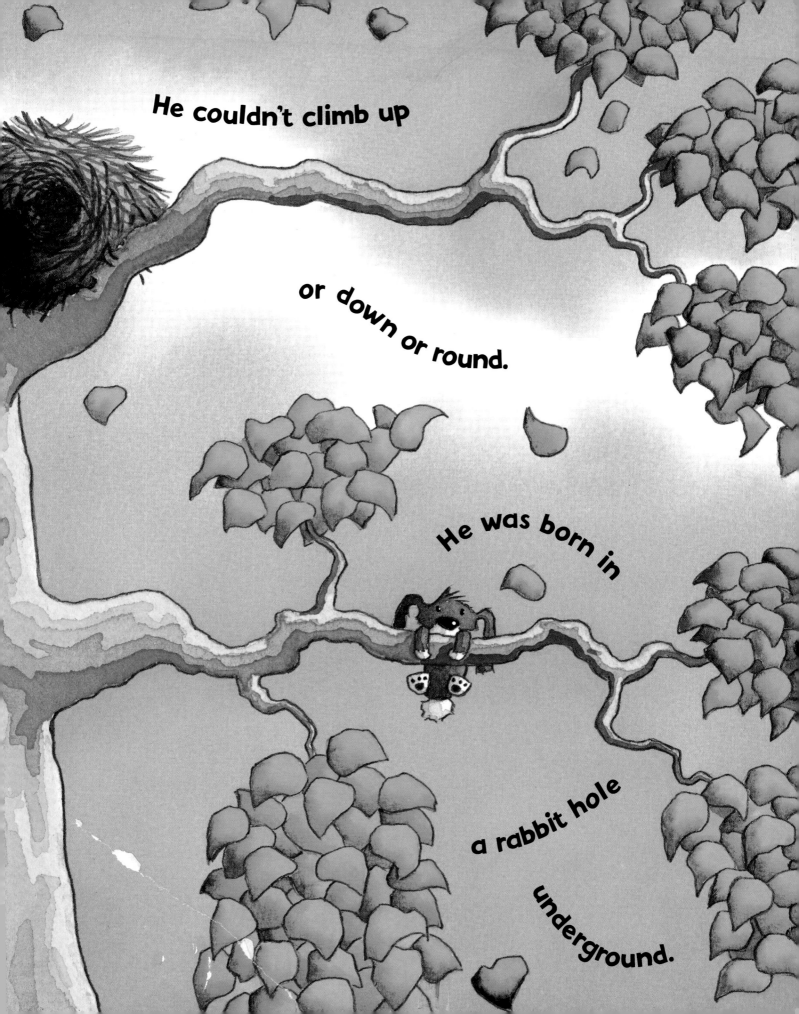

He couldn't climb up

or down or round.

He was born in

a rabbit hole

underground.

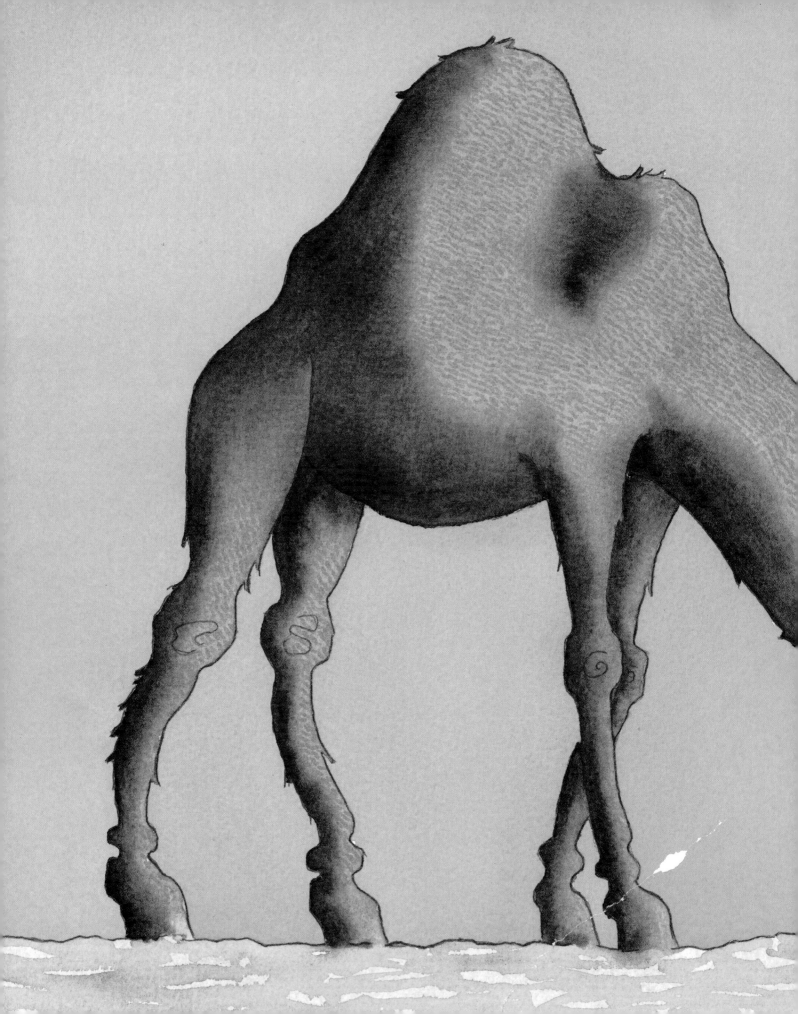

Polar Bear landed in the desert sand.
Poor Mummy Camel couldn't understand
Why he had the hump and growled a lot.
There wasn't any snow. He was far too hot!

Baby Rooster flopped into Mummy Owl's tree,
He woke her at dawn crowing "Cock-a-doodle-dee!"

Owls sleep all morning but roosters like to play,
"Wake up!" he cried. "It's the cock-a-doodle-day!"

As for Baby Elephant and Mummy Kangaroo,
He couldn't do the kind of things a joey likes to do.

He tried to ride inside her pouch
but he was such a lump.

"Hop along!" she said to him, but elephants can't jump.

Mrs Cheetah felt that Baby Sloth was rather slow,
A metre every morning was as fast as he could go.

Mrs Sloth found Baby Cheetah really far too fast,
He ran rings around her and was always racing past.

Then the world went downside-up

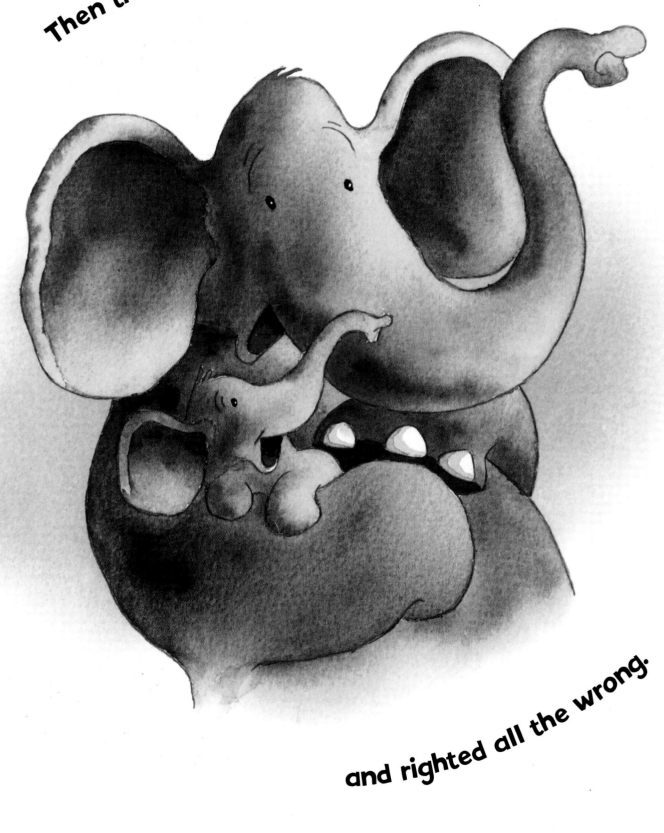

and righted all the wrong.

And now the long-lost babies
are back where they belong.

And every little creature has been comforted and fed

And cuddled by their *real* mums, who put them back to bed.

Except for two small babies who preferred their other mother . . .

So Mum kept the gorilla

and Gorilla kept my brother!

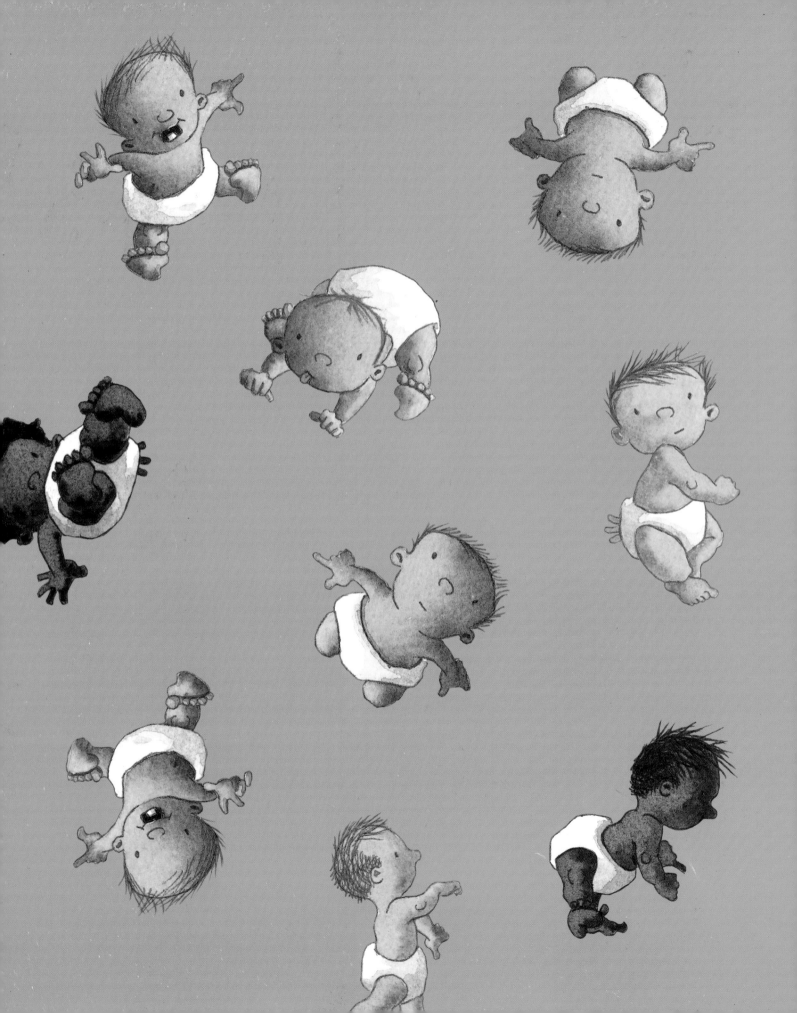

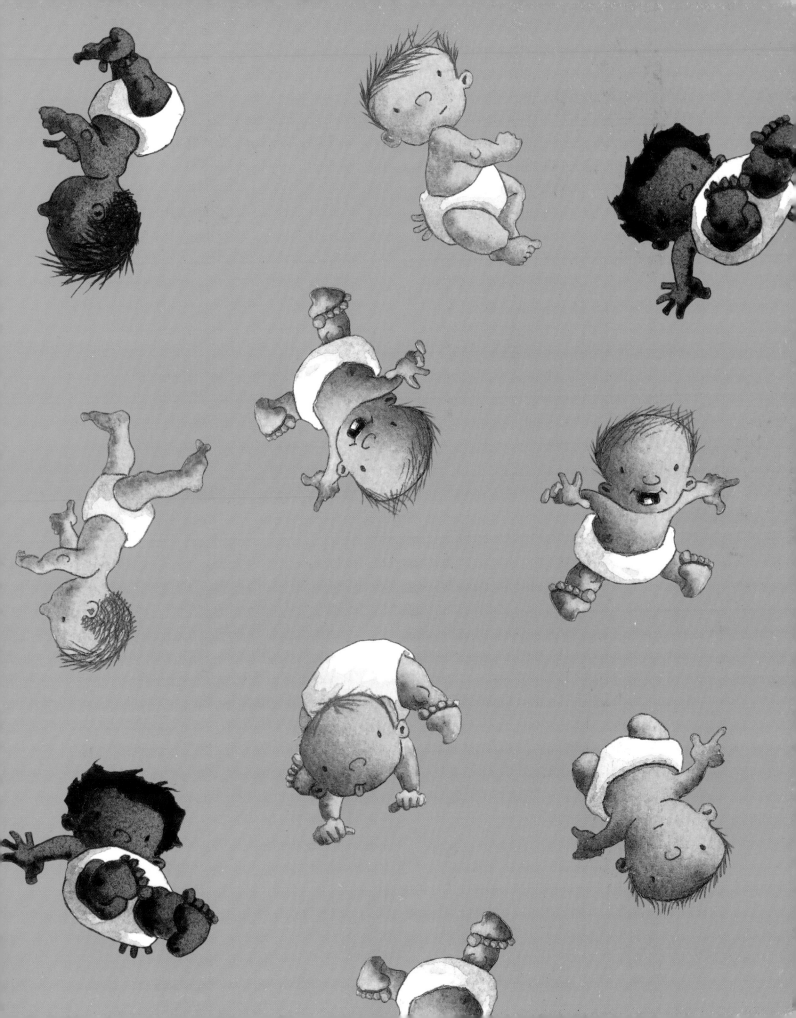

Also by Jeanne Willis and Adrian Reynolds:

9781842706985
9781842706282 (Board Book)

9781849390309

9781842709863

9781842708637

Paddington Bear

MICHAEL BOND

KT-420-197

ILLUSTRATED BY R.W. ALLEY

First published in hardback by HarperCollins *Publishers*, USA in 1988.
First published in Great Britain in hardback by Collins in 1998. First published in Picture Lions in 1999
Picture Lions is an imprint of the Children's Division, part of HarperCollins*Publishers* Ltd
77-85 Fulham Palace Road, Hammersmith, London, W6 8JB
The HarperCollins website address is www.**fire**and**water**.com
7 9 8 6
Text copyright © Michael Bond 1998. Illustrations copyright © R.W. Alley 1998.
ISBN 0 00 664716 2
Printed and bound in Singapore by Imago. All rights reserved.

An imprint of HarperCollins*Publishers*

M r and Mrs Brown first met Paddington on a railway platform. In fact, that was how he came to have such an unusual name for a bear, because Paddington was the name of the station.

The Browns were waiting to meet their daughter, Judy, when Mr Brown noticed something small and furry half hidden behind some bicycles. "It looks like a bear," he said.

"A bear?" repeated Mrs Brown. "In Paddington station? Don't be silly, Henry. There can't be!"

But Mr Brown was right. It was sitting on an old leather suitcase marked WANTED ON VOYAGE, and as they drew near it stood up and politely raised its hat.

"Good afternoon," it said. "May I help you?"

"That's very kind of you," said Mr Brown, "but as a matter of fact, we were wondering if we could help *you*?"

"You're a very small bear to be all alone in a station," said Mrs Brown. "Where are you from?"

The bear looked around carefully before replying.

"Darkest Peru. I'm not really supposed to be here at all.

I'm a stowaway."

"You don't mean to say you've come all the way from South America by yourself?" exclaimed Mrs Brown. "Whatever did you do for food?"

Unlocking the suitcase with a small key, the bear took out an almost empty glass jar. "I ate marmalade," it said. "Bears like marmalade."

Mrs Brown took a closer look at the label around the bear's neck. It said, quite simply,

PLEASE LOOK AFTER THIS BEAR. Thank you.

"Oh, Henry!" she cried. "We can't just leave him here. There's no knowing what might happen to him. Can't he come home and stay with us?"

"Stay with us?" repeated Mr Brown nervously. He looked down at the bear. "Er, would you like that?" he asked. "That is," he added hastily, "if you have nothing else planned."

"Oooh, yes," replied the bear. "I would like that very much. I've nowhere to go and everyone seems in such a hurry."

"That settles it," said Mrs Brown. "Now, you must be thirsty after your journey. Mr Brown will buy you a nice cup of tea while I go and meet our daughter, Judy."

"But, Mary," said Mr Brown. "We don't even know his name."

Mrs Brown thought for a moment. "I know," she said. "We can call him Paddington! After the station."

"Paddington!" The bear tested it several times to make sure. "It sounds very important."

Mr Brown tried it out next. "Follow me, Paddington," he said. "I'll take you to the restaurant."

Paddington had never been inside
a restaurant before, and he was
very excited when he saw
what Mr Brown had
bought him.

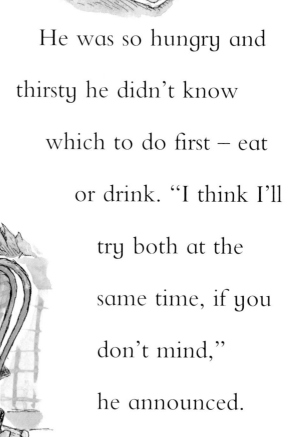

He was so hungry and
thirsty he didn't know
which to do first – eat
or drink. "I think I'll
try both at the
same time, if you
don't mind,"
he announced.

Without waiting for a reply, he climbed up onto the table and promptly stepped on a large cream and jam cake.

Mr Brown stared out of the window, pretending he had tea with a bear in Paddington station every day of his life.

"Henry!" cried Mrs Brown, when she arrived with Judy. "What are you doing to that poor bear? He's covered in jam and cream."

Paddington jumped up to raise his hat. In his haste, he slipped on a patch of strawberry jam and fell over backwards into his cup of tea.

"I think we'd better go before anything else happens," said Mr Brown.

Judy took hold of Paddington's paw. "Come along," she said. "We'll take you home and you can meet Mrs Bird and my brother, Jonathan."

Mr Brown led the way to a waiting taxi. "Number thirty-two Windsor Gardens, please," he said.

The driver stared at Paddington. "Bears is extra. Sticky bears is twice as much. And make sure none of it comes off on my interior. It was clean when I set out this morning."

The Browns climbed into the back of the taxi and

Paddington stood on a little tip-up seat behind the driver

so that he could see where they were going.

The sun was shining as they drove out of the station, and there were cars and big red buses everywhere. Paddington waved to some people waiting at a bus stop, and several of them waved back. One man even raised his hat. It was all very friendly.

Paddington tapped the taxi driver on the shoulder. "It isn't a bit like Darkest Peru," he announced.

The man jumped at the sound of Paddington's voice. "Cream!" he said bitterly. "All over me new coat!" There was a bang as he slid the little window behind him shut.

"Oh dear, Henry," murmured Mrs Brown. "I wonder if we're doing the right thing?"

Fortunately, before anyone had time to answer, they arrived at Windsor Gardens. Judy helped Paddington out of the taxi, and together they went up some steps towards a green front door.

"Now you're going to meet Mrs Bird," said Judy. "She looks after us. She's a bit fierce at times, but she doesn't really mean it. I'm sure you'll like her."

Paddington peered at his reflection in the brightly polished letterbox.

"I'm sure I shall, if you say so," he replied. "The thing is, will she like me?"

"Goodness gracious!" exclaimed Mrs Bird. "What *have* you got there?"

"It's not a what," said Judy. "It's a bear. His name's Paddington, and he's coming to stay with us."

"A bear," said Mrs Bird, as Paddington raised his hat. "Well, he has good manners, I'll say that for him."

"I'm afraid I stepped in some cream cakes by mistake,"
said Paddington.

"I can see that," said Mrs Bird. "I'd better get Jonathan
to run a bath. I daresay you'll be wanting some
marmalade, too!"

"I think she likes you,"
whispered Judy.

While Jonathan ran the water, Judy gave Paddington some soap and a towel.

But Paddington was much too busy to bother with either.

First, he tried writing his name in the steam on the mirror. Then he used Mr Brown's shaving cream to draw a map of Peru on the floor.

It wasn't until a drip landed on his head that he remembered he was supposed to be having a bath.

He soon discovered that wasn't as easy as it sounded. It's one thing getting into a bath, but quite another matter getting out again – especially when the tub is full of water and your eyes are covered in soap.

Paddington tried calling out "Help!" – at first in a very quiet voice

so as not to disturb anyone, then very loudly, "HELP! HELP!"

When that didn't work, he began baling the water out with his

hat. But the hat had several holes in it, and his map of Peru soon

turned into a sea of foam.

Suddenly, Jonathan and Judy burst into the bathroom and lifted a dripping Paddington onto the floor.

"Thank goodness you're all right!" cried Judy.

"Fancy making all this mess," said Jonathan admiringly. "Even I've never made as much mess as this! But why didn't you just pull the plug out?"

"Oh," said Paddington. "I never thought of that."

When Paddington came downstairs, he looked so clean
no one could possibly be cross with him. His fur was all soft
and silky, his nose gleamed and his
paws had lost all traces of
the jam and cream.

The Browns made room for him in a small armchair by the fire, and Mrs Bird brought him a pot of tea and a plate of hot buttered toast.

"Now," said Mrs Brown, "you must tell us all about yourself. I'm sure you must have had lots of adventures."

"I have," said Paddington earnestly. "Things are always happening to me. I'm that sort of a bear." He settled back in his armchair and stretched out his toes towards the fire.

"I was brought up by my Aunt Lucy in Darkest Peru," he began. "But then she had to go into a Home for Retired Bears in Lima." He closed his eyes thoughtfully and a hush fell over the room as everyone waited expectantly.

After a while, when nothing happened, they

began to get restless. Mr Brown coughed loudly, then

he reached across and poked Paddington with his finger.

"Well, I never," said Mr Brown. "I do believe he's fast asleep!"

"Are you surprised?" asked Mrs Brown.